The Fairies at the Bottom of the Garden

Susan Woods

illustration by
Ecaterina Leascenco

Published by Susan Woods. Printed by CreateSpace.

ISBN 978-0-646-98254-0

NATIONAL LIBRARY OF AUSTRALIA

A catalogue record for this book is available from the National Library of Australia

Dedication

This book is dedicated to little children of all ages who have big imaginations and love to see them come true in make-believe games. I also dedicate this book to my family and grandchildren Archie, Kobi, Jesse and my unborn granddaughter and to all little boys and girls who believe in fairies.

One bright and sunny morning, in the middle of the week, Sarah sat and watched her baby brother playing in the garden. Mummy was busy in the laundry and Sarah was going to help hang the washing on the line.

Baby Brother was too small to sit up, so he kicked his legs furiously and banged the mobile that was hanging on the pram. Sarah clapped her hands when he did that, and told him how clever a baby he was.

Mummy called to Sarah to push the pram over to the clothes line.

Sarah was ever so helpful, she helped mind the baby and cleaned the kitchen, and she stood on a chair to wash at the sink.

Sarah had a toy iron too, and when mummy ironed all the washing, Sarah ironed her dollies' clothes.

Sarah loved to help in the garden most of all. There were pretty flowers everywhere and a vegetable patch with lots of good things to eat.

There was one spot however, in the corner near the back-fence, that mummy never touched. When Sarah asked why, she said that it was left for the fairies.

"Oh mummy, there aren't any fairies at the bottom of the garden," and then Sarah thought; "are there?"

"Well you must be sure to keep very still and terribly quiet, and you have to look very carefully," Mummy smiled and said, "why don't you go out and see, while I feed baby his bottle".

Sarah ran through the door, then remembered that mummy had said to be very quiet. So, Sarah tip-toed up to the corner and lay down on her tummy, cupping her head in her hands and keeping very quiet and very still.

There was a large gum tree shading the corner garden and some berry bushes and a wattle tree. Wandering dew spread out like a green blanket below them and dotted in amongst it were little wildflowers of pink and yellow.

Insects buzzed everywhere, and above in the tree branches, birds chirped happily. Occasionally, a bee buzzed in and out of flowers, and butterflies fluttered up and over bushes and flowers, looking for pollen and sweet nectar to drink.

The more she listened, the louder it seemed, and the louder it got, the more it sounded like laughter. Sarah could not believe her ears. Laughter, yes, of course.

She dropped even lower to the ground, to listen. It was all around her now.

"It's the fairies, I'm sure," she said in a whisper.

No sooner had she said that, when suddenly before her eyes danced a tiny girl. She had long flowing hair and gossamer wings which fluttered busily back and forth.

Her dress was as pink as the flowers in the garden, and she sparkled like a drop of dew when glistened by the sun.

"Hello", said the tiny girl, "would you like to come and play?"

"Oh yes, I would please" said Sarah.

"Then you must close your eyes and count to three."

Sarah closed her eyes and counted. "One, two, three."

When Sarah opened her eyes, she was no longer lying on the grass, but had shrunk; it seemed, to the same size as the tiny girl, and the little garden was now as large as a forest.

"Oh, this is wonderful," said Sarah happily. All around Sarah were tiny fairy folk, little boys and girls with fluttering wings, wearing flower petals for clothes.

"My name is Apple Blossom", said the little fairy who had first appeared to Sarah. "And this is Muffin, Buttercup and Blue Gum."

Three little fairies greeted Sarah.

"My name is Sarah, and there are so many of you. Do you all live here?" she asked.

"Oh yes", boasted Muffin, a little boy fairy.

"Most of the time we live here. Of course, it gets much too frosty in winter and we go home to Fairyland until the spring."

"Let's play a game with Sarah", said Apple Blossom. All the fairies clapped their hands happily in agreement.

"What shall we play?", asked Sarah.

"Hide and seek," they all shouted happily. As soon as it was said, the fairies scattered here and there, until all had disappeared.

"Let's find them together", laughed Apple Blossom, as she lifted a fallen leaf to discover Muffin hiding beneath it. "Why, you'll have to do better than that, dear Muffin. Now come along and help Sarah and me to find the others."

"Oh twigs and sticks, it's not fair!" sulked Muffin, "I'm always the first to be found".

However, not all were as easy to find as Muffin, as they were really clever at hiding. With the help of Apple Blossom and Muffin, Sarah soon found all the little fairies.

The afternoon sun was shining through the branches above and sending warm sunbeams and refreshing the bush workers, whispering to them that it was playtime again.

"Come on Sarah", shouted Blue gum, "Let's have a slide."

Sarah watched as Blue Gum flew towards the sunbeam and climbed aboard. He let go of the sides and slid gently down to the ground. "Oh what fun" he said.

"Let's do it again", laughed Daisy, "hold onto my hand, Sarah, and now take Raspberry's hand; there, you see, you can fly to the top between us." As Sarah and the fairies played slide on the sunbeam.

Then Sarah jumped upon the sunbeam and slid all the way to the ground. Jonquil and Daisy followed her down, and Muffin helped her up.

"Oh my", announced Dandelion, a tall and pretty fairy, "we must get back to work soon, the bees will be returning to collect more pollen for the hive."

The fairies flew upward towards the blossoms above.

"How can I help you?" said Sarah sadly, "I cannot fly".

"Oh that's no problem here" consoled Apple Blossom. "I'll call Dragonfly; he'll help us".

And with that, Apple Blossom quickly flew over to Dragonfly, who had been resting in the sun and whispered in his ear, and before you could say 'Lilly pond', Sarah was harnessed to his back and flying amongst the flowers too.

Each fairy had a bag of pollen which they carried over their shoulders. They spread the pollen over the flowers, making sure there was plenty for the bees to collect for their hive.

Sarah and Apple Blossom shared a bag between them, and because they worked hard, the work was soon completed.

Apple Blossom busily collected all the pollen bags and placed them safely under a toadstool.

Apple Blossom tried to be very quick as she really wanted to hurry back and play with Sarah.

All of a sudden, Apple Blossom fell into a spider's web as she was not watching where she was going.

"Come quickly, come quickly", the ants began to squeak. "One of your friends is in terrible trouble." "Who could it be and where is she?" asked Blue Gum.

"By the toadstool under the mulberry bush," said a little ant as he hurried to catch up with his brothers.

"We are much too busy to help you. We must collect food before sundown." And with that the little ant was gone.

"It must be Apple Blossom," said Buttercup. "It was her turn to put the pollen bags away."

The fairies all rushed to her aid and discovered poor Apple Blossom all caught up in Mrs Spider's web.

"I have an idea," suggested Sarah. "If you help me onto the toadstool, I think I can help her down."

The fairies all rushed about getting ladders and ropes made from twisted grass. Sarah climbed up the ladder and onto the toadstool. She carefully stepped across and placed one foot onto the sticky web.

She held her hand out to Apple Blossom, who whimpered, "it's my wing, it's all caught up."

"Oh dear, oh dear," Mrs Spider said crossly, "do hurry up, I'm much too busy."

"Just a little more, and there... you're free" said Sarah as she pulled Apple Blossom clear of the web.

"Oh thank you, dear Sarah, thank you." Apple Blossom kissed and hugged Sarah as all the fairies clapped and cheered.

"This calls for a celebration," announced Dandelion, and everyone agreed.

All except Mrs Spider, who had her hands full, mending her broken web.

The fairies busied themselves for the party. Cups and plates were collected from under toadstools and tree roots. Honey was gathered from the beehive. Berries were picked and dew was poured into jugs. A table made from bark and toadstool legs were overlaid with petals and ferns for tablecloths.

Very soon, all was made ready for the party. Cakes, toffees and icing were made from sweet nectar.

All the fairies gathered around and Muffin, Blue Gum, Pumpkin-Seed and Raspberry played lovely tunes and sang happy songs.

It was a lovely party, and Apple Blossom made a speech in which she thanked her new friend Sarah for saving her from the dreadfully sticky web.

"Oh I have had such a lovely time, everyone", Sarah thanked them, "though I must go now, or mummy will start to worry".

"Oh yes, of course, and do promise to come and play another day", said Dandelion.

"I promise" Sarah thanked her little friends and kissed them all goodbye.

Apple Blossom took Sarah to the edge of the garden and told her to count from three backwards and she would be returned to her normal size.

Then Apple Blossom waved farewell and flew back to her friends. Sarah closed her eyes and counted. "Three, two, one."

She opened her eyes to find herself lying down in the very same spot she had been in, when Apple Blossom had met her.

Sarah hopped up and raced back to the house. Sarah thought she could hear the fairies' laughter and music all about her.

"Mummy, oh mummy, you were so right. There are fairies at the bottom of the garden."

Mummy smiled and sat down with Sarah on her knees, and listened to Sarah tell her all about the fairies at the bottom of the garden.

About the Author

Susan Woods has worked with babies and children as a midwife and nurse. A trained childcare educator, Susan has worked in several preschools in Sydney Australia.

Susan is fifty-seven, a mother of four sons, three grandsons and a baby granddaughter. Susan loves children, their love of play and sense of imagination. This book was written when her children were little and would play games in their large garden.

In the corner of that garden was a shady corner where the children would play games such as hide and seek.

Lightning Source UK Ltd.
Milton Keynes UK
UKHW050346011122
411424UK00002B/151